BIG SK

BIG SKY

A COLLECTION OF
CANTERBURY POEMS

Selected by

BERNADETTE HALL & JAMES NORCLIFFE

SHOAL BAY PRESS

First published in 2002 by
Shoal Bay Press Ltd
Box 17-661, Christchurch,
New Zealand

Cover photograph by Andrew Johnston.

ISBN 1-877251-23-2

Printed by Rainbow Print Ltd, Christchurch, New Zealand.

Contents

Publishers' Note

The inspiration for this collection of poems was *Big Weather*, a delightful anthology of Wellington poems selected by Gregory O'Brien and Louise White and published by Mallinson Rendel. We thank both the editors and Ann Mallinson for their generous permission to copy their idea, even to the extent of our choosing the title *Big Sky*, with the idea of creating a companion volume to *Big Weather*. Having taken up the challenge of matching, we trust, Wellington's wonderful celebration of its own identity, we would be delighted to pass the baton on to other regions.

The poems chosen here come from many sources and range from the extremely well known to the never before published. We have made every effort to trace and contact all the poets and copyright holders, but a few have defied all our efforts. We apologise to anyone who may not have heard from us, hope you are not too unhappy that we have chosen your poem for inclusion in our Canterbury anthology, and assure you we will be pleased to make the necessary arrangements at the first opportunity.

Introductions

JAMES NORCLIFFE

I came to Christchurch as a small boy. My childhood was spent on Mt Pleasant, on the side of the hill that overlooked the estuary and the causeway that linked Sumner and Redcliffs to the city. To get to school I walked up the hill, through Billy's Bush to Major Hornbrook Road, and on to Mt Pleasant School, which was built on a hill crest one lamp post on the country side of the city boundary, which meant we had an extra day's holiday on Show Weekend. From a group of trees known as the Seven Pines we could look down over Heathcote Valley, usually shrouded in winter in a dark smog as was the city spread out beyond. The great arc of Pegasus Bay curved past the cloud that was Christchurch to meet the jagged snow-capped line of the Kaikouras on the horizon.

Some generations earlier, Ursula Bethell from her garden in Rise Cottage in Westenra Terrace, Cashmere, looked over the city from a different angle, although her attention was more often directed to the mountains and the braided silver rivers of the Canterbury Plains. Her contemporary, the crotchety Arnold Wall, loved the hills and the mountains too. His view of Christchurch from the hills was of a 'shining city', but of course he was viewing it in a 'silvern afternoon', a rather rare silvern afternoon, perhaps. Christchurch viewed from on high usually sleeps under a blanket of grey, despite the efforts of the city council's slogan 'the city that shines', to persuade us otherwise. This sub-title, one of a succession of marketing slogans (the Garden City, Fresh Each Day), probably owes little to Wall, although it may have been prompted by Stevan Eldred Grigg's novel 'The Shining City', which used Wall's line with an irony not intended by either the poet or the marketers.

This collection, however, is not designed as a succession of hymns of praise. There is smog here as well as dazzle. Bernadette and I chose poems for a variety of reasons, none of which we really articulated. But these unspoken reasons would have included, above all, genuine poetic quality. We wanted poems that possessed originality, imagination, and delight or power in language. Of course, there had to be a sense of location, although not necessarily particularised. In addition, our tastes probably tended at times towards the quirky and the witty, even the wicked, although we didn't find too many of these.

Only rarely did we deliberately solicit poems from local poets. We did not want this collection to be a set of tailor-mades. Instead we scoured the published record, the books and journals, for the poems that would sit together in the various sections we had designed. Two things resulted: first, we found that we were able to bring to the picnic many older poets who have been somewhat forgotten by taste and fashion; secondly we found poems written by different writers and at different times which we were able to juxtapose so that they could comment and reflect on each other.

Christchurch, to the outsider, appears to be relentlessly flat. To those accustomed to negotiating the hilly streets of Auckland, Wellington or Dunedin with their winding up hills and down hills and constantly changing vistas, Christchurch can also be relentlessly boring. Not even the pretty twists and turns of the Avon or Heathcote can obviate this. However Christchurch does have its Port Hills which wrap around its south-western rim. We wanted to start with a section of poems that spoke of these hills and the mountains in the distance before we came to the city itself, hills and mountains made more precious because of the flatness of the city and the plains.

The second section deals with streams, rivers, estuaries, lakes, harbours and the sea. Thus the estuary, the Waimakariri, Waihora or Lake Ellesmere, and stretching as far as the Onawe Peninsula in Akaroa Harbour and Lake Sumner in the High Country.

In the third section we bring together the plains themselves as hinterland and something of the gardens that have given Christchurch its character. No poetic survey of Christchurch could ignore the weather particularly its nor'wester and its 'mighty arch', as it is described here by Basil Dowling. Despite this, Christchurch's prevailing wind does in fact come from the south as Ursula Bethell reminds us. Canterbury's extremes are noted by the inclusion of John Allison's poem about snow in West Melton and Joan Drewery's poem about drought.

The final section brings us into Christchurch itself, both past and present. Appropriately, it is a section including people as well as places: the welfare guy, a small Asian woman, Father Jim, and Ngaio Marsh. And the places: Cathedral Square and the museum, of course, but less obvious places as well: the Sydenham Cemetery, the Waltham Overbridge, the Clarendon Hotel and Waimea Terrace.

We have gathered together an eclectic set of poems. In turns affectionate, critical, cynical, open-hearted, public and personal, but always, we trust, striking and memorable and together, in their pointillist way, painting a composite portrait of the city and its surroundings, a portrait that reflects the feelings of those who, in different ways and at different times, have been shaped by this region.

BERNADETTE HALL

It has taken me quite a few years to become adjusted to the notion of being a plainswoman. With the kind of nostalgia that I associate rightly or wrongly with Celtic blood, I have turned automatically to sedgy, damp, haunted gullies like that of North East Valley in Dunedin and to soft hills like Flagstaff or Swampy when defining the inner terrain of my imagination. Drama lay in little wedges of sky seen through branches; sleek silhouettes with the sky flaming behind them.

However, especially after I had spent some time in the American mid-West, the notion of being a plainswoman began to take hold of me. It was as if I had shifted my campsite from a shadowy, secret river bank to a broad alluvial plain: big sky, the earth laid out below a wide horizon. There were the snow-covered mountains, the steep, crenellated rim of a volcano, a long jade harbour. It was as if I had finally opened my eyes and found I was at home after all.

Sifting through the poems in this collection has been as pleasurable for me as wheeling along on my new green bike, through Mona Vale, along the Avon, around Hagley Park. There is no escaping the weather on these plains. The wind can whip in all directions at once. A dry river bed gouged out by a glacier lies under my house. One winter there was ice on the inside of our windows. This is, after all, the jumping off place for the Antarctic. The seasons are dramatic. The city, scoured to the bone in winter, explodes in blossom in the spring. The poems in this book remind me that others over a long period of time have been equally affected by the scale and drama of this Canterbury landscape.

The collection is also about people. And there are all sorts here: artists, farmers, politicians, travellers, gardeners; enthusiasts and moaners; lovers and mourners. Maybe, in fact, Christchurch should be known as the city of poets. After all, many of the poems Jim and I chose were first published in *Takahe*, a literary magazine founded in this city more than ten years ago and still going strong. The Canterbury Poets Collective has been a focus for writers and readers for at least the same period of time. The Christchurch *Press* is, to my knowledge, the only newspaper in the country that publishes a poem every week in its book page, and has done so for the last three years. And the Caxton, Hazard and Sudden Valley presses have all been essential in the broadcasting of southern voices.

It has been fun working on this project with David, Ros and Jim. And I am proud of the selection: it is not a safe, restrained one, reliant merely on well established writers, though many of these do indeed appear. There are some here who may have had only one poem published in their entire lives and that was the one we wanted! Hopefully readers will enjoy the big embrace of our choices, as big as the sky. And if reviewers are braver than I have ever found them to be, this eclecticism will be seen as a strength. And a celebration.

PART 1

The hills that slap around my heart

Pause

When I am very earnestly digging
I lift my head sometimes and look at the mountains,
And muse upon them, muscles relaxing.

I think how freely the wild grasses flower there,
How grandly the storm-shaped trees are massed in their gorges,
And the rain-worn rocks strewn in magnificent heaps.

Pioneer plants on those uplands find their own footing,
No vigorous growth, there, is an evil weed;
All weathers are salutary.

It is only a little while since this hillside
Lay untrammelled likewise,
Unceasingly swept by transmarine winds.

In a very little while, it may be,
When our impulsive limbs and our superior skulls
Have to the soil restored several ounces of fertilizer,

The Mother of all will take charge again,
And soon wipe away with her elements
Our small fond human enclosures.

URSULA BETHELL

You Are Here

Enigmatic messages from mountains
are in themselves an answer.
This early, among the dot-dash
droplets of ice on the bending grass,
there is the language of feet
where the hare
is a soft explanation in the snow
and our boots go towards a happy end
which is always someone else's story.
There is no wind to speak of
except in whispers from the north,
overheard when the water no longer talks,
no longer says what you already know
somewhere in the blood.
At the pass the sign says
'You are here'
A knowledge the rocks hold to,
the plants embrace the edges of this certainty.

There never is anywhere else.
Even when the door closes
and the windows bleed a meagre light
you try to hold
this last piece of the puzzle tight.

DAVID GREGORY

A Good Place

Is it peninsula & unnervingly stretch
out into a deep bay,
& with that strong hold
show a solidity,
a turangawaewae?

At the top is there a view
to beat all, from all sides
protective
& for the back too?

The conditions are clear —
lives will depend on it.

Water on this side,
water on that;
a spring here,
food, a beach, wood, water:

send up the lookout -
this is a good place.

RANGI FAITH

The Conversation of Things

Small birds cough
in the hollows
of trees

my lady tells
of shadows
scooped from under

the bowls of flowers
plates are cracking
in the cupboard

out of the crazy habit
and the air — I
have gone south

returning north
the hills
are the same

chestnuts
           hustling
in a high wind.

MICHAEL HARLOW

Gorge Hill

Willow wood creaked.
An orchestra of sparrows
picked up their tunes
and hovered.

Wind held an ancient rattle.
Wheat rippled.
The harvester clattered.

Far away hills
packed up their silence
and listened.

LOUISE TOMLINSON

Port Levy Hilltop

Uncoiling bracken raises
the clutched bidibid
car-high cocksfoot ripples
bees browse at clover
nesting magpies hold court
while under konini cattle stare.

Below, loomed waves
pattern the empty beach
beyond, the chunky hills
and the Waimak curling
to the vaguer horizon
clear blue in the east.

Elsewhere the sky
is slashed by a nor'west arch.
Nor'west —
how quickly the wind
wilted the flowers on your grave,
Dick. You farmed land like this.

HARVEY McQUEEN

Hill Walk

Nothing trembles to the future
these hours are grass in wind, low
and sometimes dancing,

and where the curtain blows
back at the sun-filled window
adds a dimension.

All your paths are pocketed
for sun pools for the small
growings
paths that will wear with you
to the shape of your feet
to fit now always —
to the shape of the dream trees.

From these slopes where
the wind is liquid
and the crystal sun pure to it

these hours —
the bumble bee hesitates large
on the minute flat blue flower.

HELEN JACOBS

Port Hills Mid-Summer

drought
stalks
the lion hills
heaved and humpy
brittle-brown
where bony outcrops
muscle through
their taut
and tawny skins

a thin sky
scorches
stings
the threadbare flanks
of the stricken pride
stretched prone
exhausted
summer
at their throats

GREEBA BRYDGES-JONES

Tourist Times

From the Sign of the Kiwi the view
south is across
green hills and a plain
to dull green mountains

The public sunshine beckons, implores us
to have a good time
and at the same time warns
that we watch our backs
we who have not yet cottoned onto the fact
that we're not at home.

It used to be:
cross a dusty road, leap a gate
dive for cover behind a matagouri screen
as a posse of cars clipped our heels
then in past the waterfall
and under the mountain.

These days, shrouded in sunglasses, we follow horse trails
graduates of cowboy and war comics who moved up
through New Zealand literature to a cast of thousands

upon thousands of cubic centimetres of trail
bike and lawnmower engines in full cry. After hours
trekking dusty green hills, we reach a deserted stockyard
an enclosure of desiccated animal faeces
and suddenly need somebody (sigh)
lean backs against a rock like the Metro-Goldwyn-Mayer
lionhead snarling at the trailbikes' provocation.

While some sightseers chuck
off at the landscape – which could backdrop
an antipodean *Rupert* yarn – others trade views
which overlook it, and that's surprise surprise
how the cookie crumbles.

GRAHAM LINDSAY

Flowers Track

It's hard to
make the grade
so they built a zig-zag
into the sky,

named for the cousin
you never met — not
for the shock of marguerites
and geraniums red-hot.

The kingfisher and I
from our perches
inspect the crazed
turquoise of the sea.

The poet lying
among the tall grasses is
writing it all up.

BARBARA STRANG

Fresh Bread

You walked home from the dairy
the loaf still warm
cradled in your arms
You picked at the kissing crust
couldn't resist

That afternoon
you climbed to the top of the tallest pine
rolled down the hillside till you were so dizzy
the hillside rolled down you
made daisy chains a mile long
stayed out till sunset
gulping blue sky

Ate bread still soft
in rough chunks
thick with butter
not like grandma's sandwiches
cut from yesterday's loaf
in careful thin slices.

CATHERINE FITCHETT

I would be seamstress

The streams call up the sky.
Rag ends of cloud stitch one to another
and form a gaudy quilt that drapes itself
over the island and its mercurial peaks.

The map alters.
Reference points become one tree
and the next, their roots a ladder stretching
into the underworld in a great and solemn quiet.

I climb down into the abyss.
A strange stillness forms in the tangle of roots
as if they, too, took responsibility
for the hills and the path from where I came.

TOM WESTON

South Brighton Love Song

I am enrolled with you
completely.
Your veined cheeks draw

the sea, the sky, the blue you call
gentle.
How the word fans

inside me!
Your tongue turns the air
like a gull over Banks Peninsula.

Our heels fly
high above the marram.

NICK WILLIAMSON

For a Child

Cave Rock is made of toffee
And the sea of lemonade
And the little waitress wavelets
Are always on parade
        When the cars roll down to Sumner
        On a Sunday.

The ice-cream mountain on the blue
Is free for anyone,
And Scarborough Head looms solid
As a tearoom tuppenny bun
        When mum and dad look glum or glad
        At Sumner on a Sunday.

And wistfully the children sit
While army trombones teach
That only Christ not Cortes,
Can land upon the beach
        At Sumner when the seas roll in,
        At Sumner on a Sunday.

DENIS GLOVER

Taylors Mistake

Once this ivy was part of a rock garden.
Someone sat here drinking tea
and smiled at the world.

Or was sombre, smoked a pipe
scowled at the influx and adjournment of tides —
world's push and shove. Had no visitors
visited no one, instead looked up

the skirts of old lava flows
where basalt's weathered ribs
flaked over salt crystals

and contemplated the ease
with which a fragment
like a sledgehammer
could take out the daylight.

GRAHAM LINDSAY

At Taylors Mistake

for Léone: In memory of her mother, died 1975

Go alone to those hills on the coast
to that long bay north of the port
where a ship once turned west too soon;

As the sun rusts the skyline
look down that cragged shaft
where gulls KAAK KAAK in helixes
down to dark rocks, where winds funnel,
fuming, till sea belches the last spume
of her bones on cave walls:

go now, to be brief, daughter of morning
go now, gentle, and yield your grief.

JAN KEMP

The Heroines

In my story
the heroines
will be tough cookies
stomping round hills
in gumboots
carrying fishbins
loaded with firewood
planting leeks and cauliflowers
bearing children
more alive than any
miss universe

PATSY TURNER

Bus Journey, South

Distantly the mountains stand away
radar-like tracking, cutting my ego
down to a pocket-size Gulliver-pebble.
Autumn colours: racehorses: and more
sheep.

The road straightens like an arrow.
My legs shoot out, flop, draw back
again. The bus thunders on but can't
seem to lose the fat-back gold-bearing
animals behind: too much.
Mesmerised my eyes change sides
give up.

The sun tries hard at Ashburton but
lacks feeling. The wind mouths the
stark poplars; whistles the dogs home.
I drag myself after the others to
feed; my mouth slotting a stale Sunday
railway sandwich. *Where have all the
Maori gone, for chrissake?* And I get
a hell of a feeling that if I'm caught
trapping eels under the long bridge
the mountains will rush up to stone me.

The bus takes off belching gears.
Dead leaves lying lightly by the road
rise up, pirouette and collapse in a
twinkling whirlpool of amber light.
I suck my Gulliver-pebble: spit it out
again. Too much.

HONE TUWHARE

PART 2

The ripples and the silence

from By the River Ashley

That bridge from the city, that was Waimakariri,
Greater than our River Ashley, the playground.

The rivers, over and over again the rivers
They hasten to you, look up them, in the riverbeds.
From the soft dark forest they come down,
Or from the snows, carving their patterns
Of tawny terraces they come hastening down
To where by archipelagos of silver,
Lizard twists of azure, tranced lagoons,
We hear the ripples and the silence sing together
With the small soft sighing of the tussock,
And the flax spears' rattle, and, might be, a seabird's call.
These were the harmonies, splashed often now
By sudden hue of alien weed, still beautiful.

> Too late we hear, too late, the undertones
> Of lamentations in the natural songs —
> What have you done with my mountains?
>
> What have you done with my forests?
> What have you done to your rivers?
> Too late.

URSULA BETHELL

from A Bush Section

On, ever onward and on!
The hills remain, the logs and the gully
remain,
Changeless as ever, and still;
But the River changes, the River passes,
Nothing else stirring about it,
It stirs, it is quick, 'tis alive!
  'What is the River, the running River?
  Where does it come from?
  Where does it go?
    Listen! Listen! ...

BLANCHE BAUGHAN

Home River

you could be walking along a dusty track its long blue flowers
pushing through the metal beside you.   a road almost with
sandy soil beneath, which cuts across a dry riverbed filled
with lupin & gorse & in parts the leaping traces of stoats &
feral cats by gunshot pods

*

you might be living in a different country & find your
features altered by its history, your tongue familiar with
other names, the numerals of the year too much in the
distance to be exact.   a flint by the road casts a shadow
which wavers in the heat, the white dust

*

now you're located in time & place, let's say you have a street
address − each evening you clear the mail sifting through it
for an envelope that evokes the tracks & dust of your home
river. it is always summer. a hawk circles the brittle light

JOHN O'CONNOR

Poem With Epigraph

And what is actual is actual only for one time
And only for one place   T.S.Eliot

celia plays a waltz by chopin
the image in the window looks
at me looking at the lake and
geese that wheel then descend
landing on the dark water now
my gaze travels up over pines
up the dry hillside to sunlit
cumulous cloud filmic i think
i catch myself thinking erase
the thought it is white cloud
yellow tussock and green pine
flotilla of geese mirrored in
a lake and a waltz that's all

KENNETH FEA

'Signs Taken for Wonders'*

Against the afternoon sun,
a rice paper moon
slipped as a wafer from
the lips of hills.

And both introverted
in the flat lake under
the burnt swans, those
alter egos of the English white.

How we cannot leave
this scene alone, creating
significance where we cannot
face the significance of nothing,

as down the lake the painter
makes a gesture of hills
across her canvas, as
a breeze makes a gesture

across Lake Sumner,
sweeping fragments of
some vision
against the far shore.

DAVID GREGORY

* From Homi K. Bhabha, *Signs Taken for Wonders:
Questions of Ambivalence and Authority under a
Tree outside Delhi. May 1817.*

Don't Draw The Curtains

after a print by Kathryn Madill

Don't draw the curtains
the sky is on fire
there are many hills
after the harbour
and I am very tired.

> Don't draw the curtains
> the clouds are gathering
> at the cusp of your hill
> the light is green and otherworldly
> my boat is so small.

Don't draw the curtains
the sky is wet and falling
troughed waves are the hills
that slap against my heart
there is a long way to row.

> Don't draw the curtains
> I am far from the window
> that you look through
> the view is blurred by condensation
> I search the red horizon.

You stand ready as the dark slips in.
I close my eyes to the elemental things
and drop the oars.
The glowing curtains float across the shifting floor.

VICTORIA BROOME

Windsurfing

the hills are drawing
a fine line of it

like my mouth when I'm saintly

pines clump over there
like the hairs on my strong

right arm   the choices
are always the same

for a mercenary   for a monk.

hung a bright moth
on the thin lake skin

slicing a grin

I'm still at odd angles
laid out on shifting air

hanging on to an idea.

BERNADETTE HALL

Birdlings Flat / Motukarara

it was a place of magic
                              talking stones
and unblinking lizards on the dry hills

the wind blew jackets wide open
and the cries of wild discovery away

the gravel sucked back into the sea
the marram grass lifted and fell

the old car had rolled over a road
which rolled over compacted dunes

the leaf springs groaned and the shock
absorbers were in need of glycerine

sand flew at the windscreen and flickered
there after the handbrake finally creaked

and still flickered at our eyes when
we ran from the car into the wild wind

our hair sweeping like marram grass
donkey jackets flowing laughing crying

abracadabra Motukarara
blind to the lizards and deaf to the stones

JAMES NORCLIFFE

from Quail Island   Connection

The Maori name means
                       place of seabirds'   eggs
and still at the northern point
                           wind   rips
                                          gulls'
cries
     from the cliff's throat
                          down to the gut
where harbour tides chafe
                         guano-spotted   reefs.
The quail, though, are long gone — extinct by
1875
     too tempting a morsel
(like everything else) for settlers
to resist
          (dem dry bones). Even the old
shell beds were mined for chicken
                                grit, native
flora cut back or grazed — not that it did
much good for Otamahua's new
landlords,
           Ward brothers   drowned the first year
(1851)   though at low water
you can walk right across to Potts Island
on the mainland with King Billy Island
as stepping
           stone.   Now kanuka, manuka
matagouri   slowly regenerate

(connected to the   head-bone/
                        -land/-stone) though
Moepuku's neck is studded   with lines
of migrant pine sticking up from the soil
Lazarus
    green   fingers or abandoned
spars of some great ship sailed in and beached
years before
        when there seemed   something here
worth landing for.

ROB JACKAMAN

Onawe

Here at the head
of the bay
mudflats seethe
& shimmer green
with algae rough
around the edges
of the palette

rising sharply
from the shore
Onawe
home of the wind spirit
tapu tongue of the land
once stained dark

now only eroding cliffs
& scattered kanuka
bear witness
to the ministrations
of ghosts
guarding their bones
whispering
to the crumbling rocks
laughing
at the sea

PATSY TURNER

Ebb

The estuary is mumbling to itself.
Someone's dog bounds past barking,

a wet-feather smell ebbing into salt and spray.
Your arms prickle with goosebumps, as the easterly

wraps our skirts hobble-tight around bare legs
and our footprints bloom and fade in wet sand.

I lose your voice to the breakers, turn, catch you smiling
and ache to capture this moment: your face tilted

against grey sea dusk, and the defiant purple
of thistles, flowering beyond the sand dunes.

JOANNA PRESTON

Estuary Song

the lights move on the estuary
like bodies cleaving tenderly

like torches searching for a child
like fingers painting something wild

like campfires melting in the dark
like tigers waking in the grass

like bands setting up on stage
like lyrics sounding off the page

like cells dividing to depart
like blood tracking to the heart

like rivers braiding on the plains
like people stepping off a train

like hair drifting on a pillow
like salt mapping on a window

like fireworks falling to the sea
like fragrance finding memory

like fragrance finding memory
when the lights move on the estuary

DAVE ROBERTSON

Light & silent singing

high notes riding the dazzle
          split of sun on water

     rising & sliding on white bellies of
               sea-birds ... yesterday

     I caught a melody out at Boulder Bay
     skimming the roundness of those wet
     boulders

     It pizzicatoed white spray on
                         black reef &

     long-bowed the air with
                         wings

HELEN BASCAND

Pukeko

I see you, Pukeko
striding assertively the green hollows
crossing the road swiftly, but with
high head disdain. Alert and confident
you resist the encroachment of suburbs

and predators never properly introduced
– to you. A population still despite
the May hunters, for you aren't succulent
in anybody's pot. Giant moa and giant

eagle have become thin memory, your fat
cousin is an almost extinct curiosity.
But you, not beautiful at all, are boldly
handsome in blue and red, resolute amongst

the new arrivals and protecting your right
to stand; flag of old Aotearoa. Yes, I see
you swamphen, you gutsy old-timer, and I
rejoice that you won't go down quietly.

OWEN MARSHALL

Penguins

When penguins come home in the evening
they clamber up onto the rocks
then climb up the hill to their burrows
where they take off their wet shoes and socks
and they all settle in for a natter
about the events of the day; about the fish
they have caught and the fish they have seen
and the big one that – ooops – got away.
And the moon sweeps over the headland
making silver each leaf on each tree
and deep in their burrows the penguins
are as snug as a penguin can be.
They squabble and giggle and chatter
from moonrise to moonset and then
they waddle off back to the ocean
and the business of fishing again.

FIONA FARRELL

I remember South Brighton

and we built a bonfire
      on the sand-dunes
      between the suburbs
      and the sea

and you were on the
      opposite side of the flames
      frustrated
      about some woman

and all I could hear was
      the driftwood crackling
      in the flames
      and the waves cutting
      into the land
      the cold air fingering
      our backs
      biting our necks

and to the left
      the houses against the sea-front
      looked like models
      in a dark room

and the sky was a black
      smothering blanket
      with threads of night

and the keg wasn't yet dry
        so we continued on,
        the party dregs drinking the dregs,
        washed up on the shore

and we were both hoping
        things would be better
        now we had started university

and we stayed there
        till the dawn

JONATHAN FISHER

A Lesson on the Beach

A hood of shadows
gathers on this hill
but down on the beach

I can see you
properly. I measure
distances inside jagged

seams of sea and blue
heron sky. Love
is a loose shirt

which gives me room
to track the skid
of gulls' cries

and notice small
arrivals like these
pied stilts, crisp

in pink stockings
who yap and party
on the shore.

Now I trace your
sharp prints on the
sand's grey jacket

follow wind tunnels
through bent marram
grass. My lesson

isn't difficult
I'm not needing
you today but dis

covering your
shine against rolled
leaves of taupata

JAN HUTCHISON

above the estuary

no songs of the heart
diffidence merely

the turned aside
much practised
practice of murmuring

murmuring

                 five holes
in a fluted clay bank
wide enough for a child's hand
long enough for half an arm

how those vacancies could flash
with a blue brilliance
of kingfisher

                 notes of turquoise
and flicking silver

                          but rarely

rarely

JAMES NORCLIFFE

PART 3

As the sky climbs higher

The City in the Plains

In a silvern afternoon
We saw the city sleeping,
Sleeping and rustling a little
Under the brindled hills.
Spectres of Alps behind,
Alps behind and beyond,
Tall, naked, and blue.
The city sleeps in the plain —
A flight of glittering scales
Flung in a wanton curve,
Sinking softly to earth
Flung from a Titan's palm.
In the silver afternoon
All round the shining city,
A thousand thousand sheaves
Loll in the golden plain;
On goes the stately wain
The dun hind striding by it,
Beside the elms and the willows,
Between the Alps and the sea.

ARNOLD WALL

in camera

it sets itself up
& is exactly what it appears
to be

       a river
       a shag making a totem
       of driftwood
       dry grasses crisp
       & crackling
       cicadas

it is what it wants to be
& is simply being it

       flat grey stones
       & rocks
       seedpods
       dragonflies
       willows leaning down
       to water

the nikon clicks itself to itself
and shutters it

       something
       somewhere
       somehow

              changes

MIKE MINEHAN

Canterbury on a Cloudless Day

Driving south
the emptiness of these plains
an old jacket slung
comfortably round the shoulders
green is a secondary colour
here
       paddocks are brassy yellow
       as the sky climbs higher
           into blue

WENSLEY WILLCOX

Loneliness

I was just sitting there, wandering lonely as a cloud, when
- honest to heaven – looking out of the window
I saw Elvis. I know I know, but honest to heaven
it was him – or my name's not James Brown.
There he was, just walking across the quad in no particular hurry,

briefcase under one arm, an airy spring to his gait,
his five inch DA glistening in the breeze.
But right off you could tell he was going places;
he didn't look left or right, just ahead where he was walking.
Mid-period Elvis. His leather jacket passed within five feet of me.

And I wasn't alone, plenty of students saw him too. An older one –
probably a third year – went up and shook him by the hand.
Young women clustered in groups, glancing and whispering.
A couple of likely lads snapped their fingers. There was a palpable
happiness, for once you've seen Elvis you are never alone.

He was whistling softly. Not a curl, more an expression
of frankness was pursed on his lips as he passed (I noticed
the first signs of comfort eating just starting to grace his jowls).
I couldn't quite make out the tune, but now I hear it as
the fadeout to '(Sittin' on) The Dock of the Bay' by Otis Redding.

It was autumn, the odd lost leaf left dallying in his wake
as he turned the corner by the silver birch trees.

JAMES BROWN

Leaf

write Isabelle Isabelle Isabelle
down each green strand
     of willow
down to the deepest ell
into the deep dark
     river
then draw up the bank
to grey paved street
where a tree has posted
     a letter
an autumn leaf
stamped with the
     season's promise
stamped with the
     promise of winter.

ISABELLE HUDSON

Russet Rain

I have heard it said
That you should never walk
Under a large tree in a storm
But it was magical
A downpour of rusted golden leaves
All around me
And through my hair

CHRISTINA FITCHETT

Frost

The street sweeper has not come.
The gutter is full of leaves.
The frost cuts them off the trees at night.

And all night, awake,
these facts run along my awareness like a Russian
novel building up, a dissertation on leaf, on time,

                on the grief
                of things.

The security lights
automatically on
cannot switch
                intervene.

Frost and exposure and time in the light
of the cat night,
the hunting of time
down arteries, and the dead leaves

HELEN JACOBS

Gale SSW

At midnight a fierce storm from the South Pole assails us;
Wooden house quivers, chimneys roar, windows rattle,
Hailstones clatter on glasspanes and iron roof.
Deep in our warm beds we lie awake shuddering.

Little Omi-Kin-Kan, how are you faring out there in the dark?
Do not lose heart. Hold on till daylight.
Then I will come with watering-can and a piece of canvas,
To unbind the icicles, and shield you from the impetuous sun.

URSULA BETHELL

Wild Iron

Sea go dark, dark with wind,
Feet go heavy, heavy with sand,
Thoughts go wild, wild with the sound
Of iron on the old shed swinging, clanging:
Go dark, go heavy, go wild, go round,
      Dark with the wind,
      Heavy with the sound,
Wild with the iron that tears at the nail
And the foundering shriek of the gale.

ALLEN CURNOW

October Morning

'All clear, all clear, all clear!' after the storm in the morning.
The birds sing; all clear the rain-scoured firmament,
All clear the still blue horizontal sea;
And what, all white again? all white the long line of the mountains.
And clear on sky's sheer blue intensity.
Gale raved night-long, but all clear now, now, in sunlight
And sharp, earth-scented air, a fair new day.
The jade and emerald squares of far-spread cultivated
All clear, and powdered foot-hills, snow-fed waterway,
And every black pattern of plantation made near;
All clear, the city set… but oh for taught interpreter,
To translate the quality, the excellence, for initiate seer
To tell the essence of this hallowed clarity,
Reveal the secret meaning of the symbol: 'clear'.

URSULA BETHELL

West Melton 1995

after last night's snow
the paddock is white paper

black angus cattle at the trough
form a dropped capital

a lone calf is a sub-title
its turds an ellipsis …

all writing is a contract

and a hawk skims the open
pages looking for

a signature
beneath the fine print

JOHN ALLISON

Open Field

The earth's cold sweat, white rime on the rectangular
field like beds of daisies, the moisture cool on your arms
like ointment and on your face; the trees standing around
patient as packhorses; the blue militia, the white hikoi.

Standing out in the open field, you slow your breathing,
you go deeper, blue swishes on the white sky, smooth
as the stone the little black poodle places on the polished
floor for you to throw thrillingly beyond her obsession.

The trees are heavy with green cloud, a tent you can walk
under and the light changes. You're taller, your skin opens
with little pricking sounds, up and down the airy ladder
the plucking of soft nests, like Chris's aeolian harp.

We are what we love and you love the way the painter fades
the body into the page so the paper itself becomes the skin.
The way she opens the head as you might open a field
cleanly with a spade,
the sea streaming sideways like a Ugandan postmark.

BERNADETTE HALL

Continuity

one high tensile steel wire
strained up between two waratahs
has become a self imposed authority:

      stabbing my spade (Andrew's bloody spade!)
      into the cultivated earth,
      I dig a furrow close to the wire
      planting out Pinot Noir triple 7,
      bare rooted in bundles of fifty
      from the sawdust they've wintered in:

      enough of a trench has been dug,
      set the spade aside
      pick up the next bundle,
      cut its tape binding,
      bend over — set
      each plant in its place:

      I use the spade to bulldoze the dirt
      back where it came from,
      bury the roots that've been
      exposed to the nor'wester,
      & tramp the filled trench
      to pack down the loose earth
      around each plant until
      I feel I've done enough …

tomorrow, I'll be taking Dad back
over to Duvauchelle
for Harold Haglund's funeral

ERIC MOULD

Afternoon Tea

They have bought a pony for the child; I have not seen it,
Except clearer than dawn upon my inner eye:
They have bought a small dull pony, and discuss it
At the table while the worrying sun goes down.
But then there is the affair at the last hunt, the scene,
The old man swearing before the cars and the ladies;
And the great fence where Mrs Thompson fell.

But the tea itself; I had forgotten it:
In my first rush I had forgotten the flower,
The aesthetic culmination of a civilized mind;
I had forgotten the cream cakes and the culinary art
The silver teapot and the tasteful wear,
The throbbing lifeblood of our conversation.

The sun collapses, and the leaves fall
As if there were no reason for their falling;
The sun faints in seclusion, and the old pines
Try their hardest to withhold her last jazzy rays
Lest those sipping tea should think her insane
And dissect her as minutely as the neighbour's ways.
The opossum coughs politely; some Satanic spider
Nibbles delicately at his frozen insect;
The cow lifts its tail, and the old dog
Retires behind her kennel lest the others see her.

While the silver steams and the cups clack
While the pony stands in silent tribulation:
While the world spins into darkness and the winter descends
There is afternoon tea in the drawing room
And the cackle of empty cups in an obsequious silence.

DAVID ELWORTHY

And just now

The way light swarms over
your shoulders.
The day is remarkable that lifts
the town to walk on stilts.
The sun wheels down,
windows shine.

In the crowns of flowers
small fires leap; seeds spill
in the bright air.
Like planets spinning
into sight, passatempo our bodies
turn the hours.

For love your hair sings,
and earth's curve.
For love I pour light
into your body like this —
oh, there is music to be heard,
and just now.

MICHAEL HARLOW

Canterbury Nor'Wester

The day is lit up like a theatre,
    So eyes must get accustomed to the glare
And lungs to breathe an indoor atmosphere.
    The drama's in the west: a mighty arch
Gathers the scattered gaze to where, beneath,
    The dark tragedian clouds upon a stage
Of mountains wait as if to use their breath
    Declaiming deep 'Beware the Ides of March'.
The climax soon arrives – demonic rage
    Blusters and howls. The hyperbolic gale
So furious grows, it surely cannot fail
    To blow, before the flaring end of day,
Stage, arch, and auditorium sway.

BASIL DOWLING

The Magpies

When Tom and Elizabeth took the farm
    The bracken made their bed,
And *Quardle oodle ardle wardle doodle*
    The magpies said.

Tom's hand was strong to the plough
    Elizabeth's lips were red,
And *Quardle oodle ardle wardle doodle*
    The magpies said.

Year in year out they worked
    While the pines grew overhead,
And *Quardle oodle ardle wardle doodle*
    The magpies said.

But all the beautiful crops soon went
    To the mortgage-man instead,
And *Quardle oodle ardle wardle doodle*
    The magpies said.

Elizabeth is dead now (it's years ago)
    Old Tom went light in the head;
And *Quardle oodle ardle wardle doodle*
    The magpies said.

The farm's still there. Mortgage corporations
    Couldn't give it away.
And *Quardle oodle ardle wardle doodle*
    The magpies say.

DENIS GLOVER

Rural Downturn

A five-year-old I know
has a time bomb in his head
and a 60/40 percent chance of living.
What's-her-name down the road
has shacked up with you-know-who's brother.
Rural towns ooze gossip like conjunctivitis.
They are trying to keep the chemist
from joining the row of empty shops
like an old piano with missing keys.
Rural downturn

The grass is not greener on the other side.
They're selling off sheep with new-born lambs at foot.
The wives still go to Women's Division meetings,
Apply lippy and paint on their smiles.
A farmer topped himself the other day,
But some say his wife was a bitch.
The authorities put it down as another drought statistic:
Refinancing, restructuring, removing.
Does your wife have skills?
Rural stress.

They wear swannies like a second skin,
Red bands like flippers.
There's no 9 to 5 in their contract.
Their dogs are their real partners,
The wife's whipping up a batch of scones.
No concrete city for these guys
Specialists in their field
They like a beer, a yarn with the neighbour,
A good game of footy
They're working for the land.
Rural men.

KARALYN JOYCE

Drought

These brown hills
don't speak any more
of the soaring hawk
or the scuttling quail
and these weakening sheep
are far too tame
and the small boys
who search for crawlies
in the dying creek
now wear their father's face.
He is yelling at the woman
though she's pulled turnips
from the soil
and the soup is good.
He's sorry at night —
tells her she's his sunshine.
She tallies seed and fleece

and listens for the rain.

JOAN DREWERY

Townies

Banks Peninsula is often forgotten.
It sticks out there on the side of Canterbury,
used for holidays – the bustle of Akaroa in summer –
then ignored.
Merivaliens go home to their concrete building blocks
       clumsily placed as by a child,
With the green fingers of manicured gardens clinging elegantly.
       And they forget, forget life exists
       outside their central city bubble.

When it rains they go to the mall or movies,
       but forget the cows still have to be milked,
       the lambs won't wait till after the snow.

Beyond the plum-pudding hills, Sugarloaf with icing sugar snow,
       lie the bays.
Land squadged like clay through a child's fingers.
Burnt hills try to regain cover, fighting the extremes
       of Canterbury weather.
Stock graze the tossed patchwork quilt, trapped
       by piercing nor-westers or timeless frosts.

Work continues.
Cold fingers and frost-bitten feet keep working.
On through the shop sales, the parties,
The cold wind and hail mean Christchurch can curl up by the fire
       a good book, a cappuccino.
Forget about the outside.

The drought means they just have to water the garden more,
but when the meat isn't on the table they wonder why.

LAURA JOYCE

Without Icons

Without icons from other worlds
a green box is growing
what will be trailing lobelia
blue and white
in the wrong season. Faith hangs.

An assembly of trees on the hillside
gathers monastery shadows
where everyday birds take the insects
on flight among the pillars,
hunt seedheads through the garden bracts.

The kingfisher that stunned itself
against the window
is back after several days,
observing the telegraph wire.
An ordinary occurrence of resurrection.

It is all ordinary —
a paddock of upright dandelion heads
made extinct overnight,
mountains steepling white in early morning
and who knows what conclusions by evening.

HELEN JACOBS

Plainsong I

The monkish garden seethes
the misty whorls & spires

a labiate architecture
& the child dances a slow

movement for herself
plucks skeins of fragrances

weaves airy nets. Illuminated
the bright blade of her hair

as if we were in holier times.
I sing a plain song

constructing a landscape
the whole point being

the definition of freedom.
Amber bees flick from blue

to blue something flows
silky like water

joy I suppose
& this a prayer.

BERNADETTE HALL

Not Less By Dreaming More

We dream that we can make summer
Our cloth and paper house does not fall
Even the slow death of the garden is less

Small birds singing: medlar, almond
and pine shaken into planetary explosions
of song we catch against waking

We are not less by dreaming more; on
the back wall a bell with light inside
is where there was none before

MICHAEL HARLOW

I had this vision

For some reason
when I was
in England
I had this

vision
out an upstairs window
over the tidy
gardens with their fish
ponds and pansy borders.

There I am with a spade
in my hand
standing beside the broad beans
in my black Bata gumboots.

It's a Christchurch summer
scene, a light nor-west.
Leaf curl has screwed
the nectarines, cabbage whites
skate on thin air while graceful
monarchs copulate
on the grape vine

and that sweet neighbour's
peach is lounging
on our side of the fence
above a vibrant
patch of silverbeet.

I'm all
smiles in my yellow
tie-dyed T-shirt.

NICK WILLIAMSON

Flying into Christchurch

The day's frayed cuffs
scuff on the warm earth of evening,
insisting that cycles pass, expectations slipping
out over the mountains

burning their imprint into the cloth
of the sky, vermilion,
smoke wisping
from singed fibres as light surrenders

and the week ends. Across the plains,
flat angles rather than paddocks,
gaps where there are sawmills, shingle
pits, the whole commerce of the land

reduced to one condition. The rug
of the sea is rucked up and covered in dog
hair,
unravelling at the edges where the surf
breaks onto wicker beaches. Colours shake off

so much geometry, with the rivers
carying the burden of dying light
and the braided river beads becoming horses
or violent lovers, shiny as tin foil

TOM WESTON

PART 4

In the street light

The City from the Hills

There lies our city folded in the mist,
Like a great meadow in the early morn
Flinging her spears of grass up through white films,
Each with its thousand thousand-tinted globes.

Above us such an air as poets dream,
The clean and vast wing-winnowed clime of Heaven.

Each of her streets is closed with shining Alps,
Like Heaven at the end of long plain lives.

ARNOLD WALL

The Old Provincial Council Buildings, Christchurch

The steps are saucered in the trodden parts,
But that doesn't take long to happen here;
Two or three generations' traffic starts
In stone like this to make time's meaning clear.

Azaleas burn your gaze away below,
Corbel and finial tell you where to stop;
For present purposes, it does to know
Transport is licensed somewhere at the top.

Children of those who suffered a sea change
May wonder how much history was quarried
And carted, hoisted, carved; and find it strange
How shallow here their unworn age lies buried

Before its time, before their time, whose eyes
Get back from a stopped clock their own surprise.

ALLEN CURNOW

Yet More Words...

for John Summers

That welfare guy
in neat buff trousers
leaned hard on his words
which fell in the passive lap
of a woman-husk
waiting to be shepherded
into the small carpeted
Gothic arena,
her hair of frizzed hay
haloeing the head, trivia-stuffed
like the cheap purse
from the mission shop.

It's those foster kids —
we're burning up the gas
in the middle of the road,
while they drift along the sides...
we don't leave a place
for fifteen year-olds
in our stupid big city.
They're the ones... they matter...

In the warm wind
a sombre raven in the Square
teeters... croaks
jerks his bony neck and
chest forward
pro-Police
pro-Empire
pro-Raven

words like black bats
hurl past captive Godley
garbed in verdigris.

Soft-haired, soft-tongued
the poet stands among his people
those foothills and escarpments of books.
Why does the Kiwi, he asks,
cherish this rugged masculinity —
despise tenderness?
His mildness hides Gaelic fire...

Squat red beetles
sidle away from the sacred tiles,
spangled dots above us tell
        what we've already felt —
twenty degrees.
A Peanut King gains power...

Every headline is grit in the eye.

LORNA STAVELY ANKER

Cul-de-sac with Chestnut Trees
and Small Asian Woman

Almost three months have passed
since I moved house
yet the street remains unfamiliar.

Against the bare hands of children
and my dodging feet
fruit from the trees   spikes the paths.

This morning I am brittle
like a twig.   I wonder what the season
will bring.   A woman round

the corner seems to know.
Stooping under the branches, she's slender
like a new root, and tentative.

Soon her wrists tense above
thick cotton gloves.
She edges closer to a green fruit
and ponders.

As if she reaches deeper than
its prickled shell
and scans some polished nuts that
bed inside the lining.

When she flicks back a few strands
of hair, her plait
dusts   a space between us.

It's hard, she says, *to open a chestnut.*
It takes time to peel off
its skin.   I add the pulp when I cook.

A pan of chicken pieces simmers
towards me.   I taste honey, rice
and saffron, sweet and mellow.

JAN HUTCHISON

January Child

the lawn winter green
then here she comes
'naked as' chubby feet
patter past the garage
or see thru the crosscut
wall   she might mimic
her brother and cheeky
grin dive off the settee
swim the carpet ocean
bedtime deep … here
she had bread for black
birds … for sparrows
camellia bud & flower
fall … call her 'huggle
bug' fresh shampooed
scent in her whispery
hair just a hint of birth
she with the peanut up
her nose … in a wind
slammed door lost a
fingertip microstitched
back again   her hand
bandaged up set for a
boxing glove to cope
with her brother see
her in the red checked
dress whirley Dervish
twist the air of heaven.

JEFFREY HARPENG

Flippers

An enclave of rude wee baches yells orange at us. A suburb
this well-appointed can afford to let its ghosts all swing. If this
is a backwater, then call our strides dog-paddle. We're
gurgling in these grins.

Finishes peel from weatherboard over Mix and Single
Central. Gauche enough for comfort, the old ducks' cribs
work as ovens, simmering hammocks and parrots. Down rimu,
sweat of gum marks overtime out at Indian Summer's end.

Next to the Heathcote, ripples of tarmac sway up - waves
set to breach our critical mass of vision, tsunami in mirage.

Listen. Antipodean vowels chew up your left ear, boom the
footpath. At Jade Stadium, googlies and flippers are spinning
the ockers into the pitch. The field sparkles. They dive on any
half-chance and each appeal sounds confident.

An octogenarian tests the resistance of her fence's corners.
She leans into her smile from the refinement of a Georgian
finishing school.

The neighbour's cat is coiled for spring-launch, with elm
and rata to flatten. He's on form.

Yes, it's right about now that you sprint like a carcass
blasted from a trench, sprawling in heatwaves out of the
cemetery. There's art in your munching of persimmon.

A half-light close to shade quickens, diminishes sight as we
rail against mauve pickets; our bare feet scuff at marram that
bounces like chevron.

Let's retire.

It's a crude flop down to the river. On Waimea Terrace,
beginnings will slough from our minds.

GREGORY DALLY

up on Waltham Bridge

in the wet with the light
just this way these rails
shine like snail trails

traffic crawls down the avenue
ignoring the arch efforts of Elle
McPherson to sell it lingerie

or Big Fresh mooing its wares
from its paddocks of cars
and two metre shade trees

they are dismantling Daytona Park
the wooden cactus the saloon doors
the whole painted cowboy town is

going west going the way of the gas
works the railway station
                                    the bridge
propped up and lying as languidly

as Elle has seen it all before
arches itself over the shining steel
allows things to creep over it & under it

and for the moment doesn't flinch
despite the dusty tumbleweed
and the grit in its stunted pines

JAMES NORCLIFFE

A Suburban Street Sonnet

this afternoon the old gaffer's
talking to my neighbour, all about

the lilacs and wisteria, and just
how wonderfully they're blooming;

and Father Jim comes by, whistling
the Spinning Wheel, admires

the garden and the lovely weather
while the foot's stirring, must

keep going. got to call on Mrs Cox
the widow (now the foot turning

over stones in the dust) it's nice
the way those banksia roses swarm

across that trellis, and the feathers
of that tamarisk amid the toi-toi

(and over the street, the sweet voice
of a young maiden, singing).

JOHN ALLISON

Ae I Eye

In postures of mischievous mockery
I strut the streets of Otautahi
The people I see seem stuck like trees
So high I float by like a summer's breeze

In times of thought I think of all the clones
A plight of people prepaid like phones
In dark empty streets exhaust fumes and chrome
Consecrate the concrete; this is mai home

Christchurch city scape skies forecast is gritty
Buildings wire buzz bleed electricity
Questions: Kia Ora Kia Mate
Searching for Waiora a Tane

Allusions; construed hope in a world of sin
Four aves and these Botanical gardens

TIM WHALE

Recordings

Rain tickles that dark remnant inside me.
I tune in to water yodelling down the drain,
imagine the happiness of trees,
the happiness of water.

A bell chimes, far away, eight times,
one sound after another.
Some hoon plants his foot on Bealey Ave.

Cave drawings engage me.
Hi-glo pink, yellow, orange, blue, the mark
of an earlier man trying to cheer the place up.

These days slime is reclaiming the walls,
silencing those vivid celebrations

drowning his wild snakes and dancing men.

Here I am, naked as a prune in water.
Fifty-two
and just beginning.

NICK WILLIAMSON

from The Sunshine Factory

I

Here come the subdivisions, swallowing the farmstead,
the spinning gums, bronze flax and butterflies
closing round it. Everyone's off

to the country it seems, and this is how far
we've got - even though our
hearts keep retiring ahead of us, westward, always

towards the mountains, out across those opulent
acres of wheatfield and orchard. A patchwork
inhabits our dreams, a stitching together

of mutton-fat furrows and kiwifruit,
jet-boats, the silver flood
bulging with salmon, and the A-frames and rancho-style

sea-shells and stucco fan outwards, the Casa
del Kowhais, yards of plate-glass
brilliant with echoes of the powder snow that lies

like icing on the Alps.
Here we are then
on our way to the country: why, only over the road,

in the paddock by the Sunshine Factory, a girl is out
cutting caulis in bright yellow leggings and pretty
red gumboots, her breasts swinging

free in her bush-shirt, bathed in the promise of fruit loaf
warm and yeasty. The cream and golden stacks
of the bakery tower above the succulent loam,

gleaming like mountains, and the dry breeze
that wafts off the Plains blows
softly in the ear of the city, breathing that salutary

smell of bread into our homes.

JOHN NEWTON

Sunset

The whisky in the crystal
tumbler on the workbench

is the same colour as the sun
on the hills – two old fools

who pull me to the door, the gate
down the street to where

on a gentle rise on the plain
in the middle of Sydenham
Cemetery, I'm surrounded

by a bunch of aged grey concrete
in memory of who knows who
who fell asleep in the hope

of resurrection, of eternal life
plus the usual arbitrary
dates of death our own will echo.

A hair's breadth, a breath away
from death, I watch

the wounded hero sky go out
in a blaze of glory

out past the little gardens of the bodies
beyond the clutter of broken masonry.

Sunset over the baked clay
roofs of Spreydon.
All this beauty fading away.

GRAHAM LINDSAY

Avon River at Carlton Mill

on slippery grass moist shod beside the river
they take their daily walk   a woman and her dog
trees in their ordained disorder blanch
and tint their leaves then loose their hold
as if the sunlight falls in tumbling pieces when the wind blows cold

duck-brown ducks with ballerina eyes
dive below the oaks   as acorns fall
slick slipping water gleaming clear
glosses stones entombed beneath
as if the careless river's never known a single moment's grief

through xeroxed days of desolation grief's dull
footfalls mark her path   a woman bereft
the symphonies she heard with him have ceased
their music lost in sorrow's sighs
as if all songs are sung on distant mountains when one's lover dies

she doesn't see the trout below the bridge
finning in its lair   she turns for home
the dog looks up – he knows their walk is done
another dawdling day has passed
as if they hope this lonely walk this autumn day will be their last

BARBARA McCARTNEY

Eclogue: Christchurch in Winter

Ultima Cumaei venit iam carminus aetas:
magnus ab entegro saeclorum nascitu ordo.
                                    Vergil, Eclogue IV

In Te Wai Pounamu, winter comes in hard
straight off the Antarctic ice floes, scything low
over the flat scrub of the plains & outside
the sheltered harbours Tawhirimatea of the storms
lashes at
Tangaroa's glum lead waters with his fists. In
the wet black sand, the godwits print angelic biographies
with their bird-foot cuneiform before
they take off for the warmer lakes of Siberia.

North Hagley Park smokes like an old piece
of roof tin chucked on a tip fire,
with the breath of people & bare willows
in this grey steel freezer of a South Island cold snap.
Joggers & dogs towing their people cough up
expanding gypsophila blooms.

Far out, resting on the surface of the nation
of groper, terakihi & the ugly roughy, a Russian
trawler captain looks to an angry black horizon,
dreaming of a bountiful catch.

The office lemming plucks a file from the cabinet,
delicately like Orpheus strumming his lyre. He looks
out into the raw grey day &
moves closer to the radiator.

As soon as afternoon tea is over, darkness falls.
Spring becomes
a bitter aftertaste & talk of cherry blossom
drops out of frequency. The Southerly chooses to whistle
a subzero tune from the Ice Age's greatest hits
until my cheeks burn like beetroot.

The streets are stuccoed, candy-coated –
Jack Frost's crack troops
are parachuting in through a sky dirty white on white:
Scandinavian snipers
in Arctic camouflage,
a charcoal picture, the trees are by Mondrian.

This monochrome remains
even after I shut my stinging eyes.

ANDREW PAUL WOOD

Bridge of Remembrance

Whoops! Steady on. Steady...
For a moment there
it almost got hold of him:

the setting sun, pulling like this
quiet whoosh of water
downstream from the bridge

and underneath his diaphragm
he'd felt a draining out:
the sad incontinence of memory

> *Singing in the ear.*
> *Like angels, blooming*
>
> *angels, made audible*
> *through a miracle*
>
> *of tinnitus. Alamein.*
> *Dawn. The batman*
>
> *having time only to*
> *sandbag his captain's*
>
> *side. The mine.*
> *That bloody mine...*

Not yet. Not yet, that sinking
in the current, sucked
into the vortex of the sun.

(These are my father's words
and mine I hear while
sitting in the cafe, sipping

at a cappuccino.) The old man
turns and very slowly
wades back into his shadow.

JOHN ALLISON

Yeats in Clarence Street

At midnight on the council pavements
                              Riccarton
exposes its midweek skull: the air is full
of drizzle and suburban gothic. A desultory
neon sign   fizzes
                              red omens but there's
nobody there to see or hear
                              the takeaways
cook sharpening his kitchen knife. As I walk past
I'm not aware that in the small hours he'll chase
his boyfriend down the street and into my
garden
          rampaging outside until I give
the poor lad sanctuary. The cook is a
very large man
              — even larger as he stands
in starlit silhouette down my hallway.
Never much given to religion, now
I feel the urge to pray
                        and the boyfriend
prays too   and sure enough in the end
the man outside gets bored and pausing only
to decapitate an innocent
                              rhododendron
goes about his normal work
                              (still wiping
the knife on his sleeve with a
                        backward glance).

The moon makes mosaics from the leadlight
windows in my lounge; the fury and mire
lapse back into blood   slowing the doomed
heart; though
                    by Lyttelton   dolphins are
tearing the sea to poems scattered across
the tide.

from 'Rockyhorrorton (Riccarton Revisited)'

ROB JACKAMAN

Developing My Father

My father has been enlarged
in a Sydenham photo shop

specialising in reproductions
and silver fish repair.

He walks with my mother
down Hereford Street.
She wears a hat and tender gloves.

He wears a striped shirt, the collar
splayed like the wings of his RSA badge.

There was a war to put behind
them; shopping to do, hungry
mouths to feed.

The street photographer shoots them
wide-eyed under a white sky.

For years he stores the negatives.
My mother and father
holding hands in the dark.

FRANKIE McMILLAN

My Aunts in the 1960s

There are Cissie and Myra
in Cathedral Square.
Cissie thinks they were
on their way to work,
they walked in from Lichfield Street.
It was summer, anyway.
They are standing in the shade
in black and white
behind the Cathedral,
the big English trees
reflect in Cissie's glasses.
Myra has on a white hat
and gloves and wears her pearls.
'Oh, she liked to be all get up
and go out', says Cissie,
'all I needed was one good frock'.

VICTORIA BROOME

The Royal Visit

I suppose we cheered as she went by
Elizabeth & consort
Christchurch, early '50s.

I know for sure it was Lincoln Road,
by the racecourse
& comically at this point

an old man driving a horse & cart
preceding her
by a minute or two

to my mother's dismay who was always
wondering what
the neighbours would say

& the old fellow the errant father
of someone or other
policeman, politician

someone 'of standing' who would
be *shamed*
later we gathered

at the Clarendon Hotel where she stayed,
& I remember
seeing my father

crossing the street, surprised that he looked
so shameless
before the crowd.

like an old photograph, the women & men
ordered, overweight, in coats —
all the men wore hats.

JOHN O'CONNOR

First Perceptions

We'd never heard of Kate Sheppard that summer.
        The summer of red-raspberry lips and hands and
        carrying buckets of scarlet delight to the kitchen
        jam-factory. And the men drinking beer on the verandah.
        And Grandad laughing and somehow looking bigger with
        his family around him. And Molly who wouldn't play with
        us any more, slyly hitching her skirt to show the shine
        of knees in her new nylon stockings.

And Uncle Jack who was too clever by half according to Dave
        sprawled in the doorway, doing the crossword puzzle.
        … climbing giggling over his legs. Watching his
        palindrome eye casting between verandah and kitchen

        dark-hot kitchen… hot fat bodies
        in floral dresses; hot jars on white wooden table;
        burning black stove and black pot boiling deliciously,

        dangerously.
        And Aunt Mary crying.
        And Mother saying: there, there, and: I'll skin you
        kids alive if you don't get out from under my feet.
        And Aunty Mary, stirring the cauldron, saying:
        I've fallen in again. And young Tom snorting: Bollocks!

        She wouldn't fit in that pot.

And knowing he was right. You see, there wasn't a mark on
        her blue dress.

JOY LOWE

Sleeping Over

crickets fall all night
                against a dirty sky
we lie

covered with a sheet
                and each other
sleep torn

in places by car stereos
                we surface now
and then

to breathe in street light
                test the orange air
for uncertainty

SARAH QUIGLEY

Party Tricks

for Jules

it pays
to have a party
trick or two
tucked up
your sleeve
like Patrick's
pavlovas
or his blood
red T-shirt
with the white
blazon BETRAYAL
& you did brush
out your long
blond hair
for that boy
(I know I know,
he was a real dick)
& people did stare
at the pair
of you &
an American said
in a big voice
outside Le Café
in Worcester
Boulevard,
'My God, boy,
you look just like
Tom Cruise!'
which was true

& the police
bugged our house
you said
because he was
dealing but
nothing can go
too wrong
I say
for a girl
who can raise
one scathing
black eyebrow
higher than
the other
& talk
like
Donald Duck

BERNADETTE HALL

The secret life of Arana Kohu Rau

His daddy was the Anglican minister at Lyttelton
when little Allen wandered away in the midst of
one interminable sermon too many and ended up
as whāngai amongst the Ngāti Wheke at Rāpaki.

Presumed drowned, the little Curnow became
someone completely other: Arana Kohu Rau,
the child of a hundred mists. He browned up
well in the harbour sun, soused in te reo 14/7.

At school he was told he would be a bulldozer
driver or perhaps with luck, a gun shearer. Now
Arana knew he was meant for greatness, so he
kicked the teacher's shins and became delinquent.

With English as his second language, Te Kohu Rau
was double crippled but sang with such a weird
intensity, he was permitted to work on the roads,
practising his English consonants, his z's. his y's?

Other boys might go in jackets to the great Boys'
Highs. Arana Kohu Rau was meant for war — and
to war he went, for Te Kuini, Te Karauna, blood
to spill for nothing in the haka roar: ka mate, ka ora!

Arana stormed Cassino and came back deaf.
Most of his mates lay in the rubble, dead.
Arana saved his world and came home mute.
He had all of a life to tell and none could hear.

He fell to a heart attack in 1964: at his tangi
many of the fiery speeches blamed the war.
At Rāpaki, there on the harbour's shore
the cries went up, the tears rained down

As Allen's ghost rose wading from the drowned
volcano's cone: 'I've got a national literature
to found: for God's sake, take me home to Daddy!'
And Arana? He strides the hills alone, chanting this

ancient oriori: the tupuna sang to their own.
'Kua riro te whenua, e tere ra i te moana ei!'
'The land is gone, it is drifting out to sea!'
and he does so thanklessly, for you, and for me.

JEFFREY PAPAROA HOLMAN

Note: 'Te Kohu Rau' means 'one hundred mists', which we know as
the Pākehā version, Kurow. The quotation in the final verse is from
'E, i te tekau mā whā' (tribe unknown). Translation by Margaret Orbell
in *The Penguin Book of New Zealand Verse*, eds Ian Wedde and
Harvey McQueen, Penguin, 1985.

The Skeleton of the Great Moa in the Canterbury Museum, Christchurch

The skeleton of the moa on iron crutches
Broods over no great waste; a private swamp
Was where this tree grew feathers once, that hatches
Its dusty clutch. and guards them from the damp.

Interesting failure to adapt on islands,
Taller but not more fallen than I, who come
Bone to his bone, peculiarly New Zealand's.
The eyes of children flicker round this tomb

Under the skylights, wonder at the huge egg
Found in a thousand pieces, pieced together
But with less patience than the bones that dug
In time deep shelter against the ocean weather:

Not I, some child, born in a marvellous year,
Will learn the trick of standing upright here.

ALLEN CURNOW

Large Soaring Bird

based on a sculpture by Bing Dawe

majestic even in death
    bones blackened by the sun
white down once
        an aurora to the wind
            now stripped
brake cables flap
    wing bones broken
yet you soar
        above kauri
            marlin twine
                and cycle parts

JANE SIMPSON

Two Pictures by Van der Velden

Funeral in Winter

Not the coffin skimming the snow
the procession bending against
the invisible wind or beyond
the sextons leaning on their shovels
the glow of their pipes
a small joke in the raw landscape.
What we see is the black and white
of it all. The moment in
lovemaking when we're quite
alone. The flame running
its index finger around
the glass's rim

Otira Gorge

The civilised eye torn
from its socket so savagely
does the water shoot
the painter's *wine dark*
rapids. It's not the place
to advertise filter tips
but you can see the love
in it. Those dark moments
when we retrace our steps
see ourselves as we are
in that light they wouldn't
advertise tampax
either.

HUGH LAUDER

At the white funeral in Marken

Your shoes are full of snow
Peter van der Velden
but you stay out
of the picture
for hours.
(At home on the hearth
water is singing in the kettle.)

You left the anonymous villagers
to warm your feet.
In their black mourning.
They strain into the wind.
They carry the rectangular wooden box
to a dark hole sheathed in white
out of the picture
while you paint your bold name
weeks later
under their grief.

How could you have left them there?
How could you have come here
and sat for hours
at the base of Otira
you self-indulgent
man?

KOENRAAD KUIPER

Death in the Family, 1982

1 Dame Ngaio Marsh

*Music. The Performer stands in front of an illuminated
photograph of Dame Ngaio Marsh.*

I don't know if you followed cricket;
Saw how, with an English tingle,
It hangs its suspense out over our summer days.
Longer even than your crafted thrillers.
Catches are held like clues:
The thwack of ball on bat
Leaves a red stain just like the butler saw,
Or the vicar on the village green
Holding his cup out absent-mindedly for tea. *(Music ends.
Performer sits, with a cup in his hand.)*
Stretching the point:
You had, as they say, a good innings.

I've read the perorations (as one does)
Made my own adjustments (as one must)
Pictured you dying with panache
Like the good sport you were:
'Got out flashing at a wide one,
A thick outside edge and she was gone –
You could hear the roar far from Lancaster park.'
Hearts quickened in London.
Clocks stopped in our dark.

Could at this point roll you into the general lard:
'With this dismissal we are all the poorer.'
'We shall not see her like again.'
'Yes, I was gratified to touch her hem,

I knew her lonely, great, and now amen.'
Let others rub her out the more they praise her
I come to bury Ngaio, not erase her.

(Performer moves back to address the photograph.)
And so a paragraph of history.
A grape or two soured in ingratitude:
You were of your place and of your time,
Born to stand above the stagnant pool
Of Christchurch.
Still you breathed her air,
Agreed with her that art is imitation,
Its bright suns not rising on these colonies
(Where nothing of urgency could ever happen)
But on universals distant as exiled prisms.

(Music.) Glib as the nib of a Conway Stewart
Suspense poured out of you,
Drunk at night like Ovaltine.
Christchurch and the Empire slumbered on. *(Music ends.)*

In the theatre it was much the same:
You pared the plays down, made thrillers of them,
And then within the limits you had set
(For bank unversed antipodean minds
Three centuries and a hemisphere from Home)
Worked like the great conductor that you were
To give us the 1812 complete with cannons.
We called it 'Shakespeare' and were thrilled to bits
That we had 'culture' here on God's Own Swamp.
(The performer has moved away from the photograph.)

O that dash, that get-up-and-go!
O that Heraclitean flow!
All Australasia called you Caesar!

We called you God! Your house,
A modest mansion on the Cashmere Hills,
We pictured as a temple, approached in fear.

from Passing Through

MERVYN THOMPSON

Sonnet XVIII *from* Lyttelton Harbour

Farewell Cathedral City! — and its Square,
Its Founder foundering in a pot of tar.
Farewell you City Fathers! have a care
Tho' you be down'd you not yet feather'd are.
Rogues are anointed here, the blest afar.
Farewell fond river and its gardens fair!
Watch how my name above you like a star
Points but to one remember'd entrance there,
Not to its classrooms and their frequent bell,
The doorway to a world I now explore,
But to the fields where I might not excel,
Whose bright, brief laurels have I lov'd the more.
You fateful leaves! Not you I bid farewell,
But pluck you now, as I might not before.

D'ARCY CRESSWELL

from Self-Criticism of an Otago Poetry Worker

Abel Tasman, I salute you,
sailing these frigid cum tropic azure zones
from which would later spring such memorabilia
as whalers, nuclear testing, high-tech tourism –
the poisonous fruits of the Imagination,
The lost Elysium's England, they said, driving to Blenheim.
Newsreel spectres jog the elbow of Memory.

Boats pitch forward to Resolution Cove.
A small Honda winds past, tooting its sullen horn.
Inflation cycles from chainstore to chainstore.
In her make-up she shines like a mandarin slice
on a choice cheesecake, spreading illuminations.
Oh to live on beaches by the crash of waves,
solarizing with a brunette beside the polystyrene flotsam
of a picnic lunch, our wrinkly togs held up with elastic,
bladderwrack going pop.
The heroic ranges and the Empire of Sheep! We may never get
        another chance is a phrase never far from our lips.

O Christchurch, I can see how the flagrant heat sometimes wins
        you away
from that curious glacial pose in which so much absence
        is suggested.
Ah stung vanity, ah slippery efforts to have congratulations
        accepted.
The stone lids of Time will lift when everything has crumbled.

Those doomed splendours,
the dark hydrangea flowerheads, are radiant symbols of mortality.
This tattered foliage is otherwise harmless.
A reporter takes the fakes down.
Coal-black water springs back
its tense, soft skins,
curling under thin, slanting rays.
Light collects on the wing of the moth
and disappears into the brown monotony.

DAVID EGGLETON

Christchurch

This town knows me. It
has in fifty years become
as familiar as the smell of
new babies, minted lamb,
fresh mown grass and the
icy winds off the Alps.

This old Cortina knows me.
It weaves past the Takahe
like a well-oiled actor
rattling along full of children
and groceries into the
city of committees.

This town knows me. It
gives me a wide berth
and tolerates my unorthodox
comings and going
It knows the beat of my being
and flowers in my mind.

How simple is the real state
The single petal, the black shag,
The small child bending
a thread of patterns
all different and yet the same —
linked.

JENNIFER BARRER

Christchurch, NZ

I have just flown 1100 miles from Australia
& landed in a Victorian bedroom
They sent up cindered muttonchops for lunch
There is an elderly reporter with pince-nez
He wants to know why I have sideburns
& if I dont think being patronized by the Canada Council
isnt dangerous for my art or dont I feel I need to suffer?
In stone outside my window Capt. Scott
is nobly freezing to death near the South Pole
Suddenly I know the reporter is right
Sideburns have been sapping my strength

EARLE BIRNEY

from Professor Musgrove's Canary

*

Now are you sleeping? Half-frozen
One minute, hot the next
With no leg room and airhole blanket.
Be calm. Think of Oates
Or better Robert Falcon Scott
Imagine his mother calling him that
The wonderful naming qualities of mothers
Some goof of course but many get it right.
In Christchurch recently I stood in front of
R.F. Scott and thought of her calling
Softly *Falcon* to him at an early feed.
My Falcon. Spoken by falconress.

*

Not
what
we
wish
but
turning
what
is
to
its
beauty

*

Is formal just a merge
Carried to microcosm
The same two-way passage as with words
The ship of hopeful hearts stuck in ice
Setting up a smithy and working out the rations
Then the rations were themselves.
A diary note: the fated Falcon wrote
'I am proud to know there are still Englishmen...'

If only his mother had called him Sparrow

ELIZABETH SMITHER

Heading Hoon Hay

to Christchurch
from the north
if you don't care how
drive down the plains
through dusty
Waiau
  Waikari
   Waikuku
Why then
over Waimakariri
by bridge, not ferry
Cathedral Square
But you can't park here
So it's Riccarton
Islington
  Templeton
    Rolleston.

Try Christchurch
from the west
with a clear blue sky
down from the Alps
to travel
right by
Springfield
  Sheffield
   any field?
   Darfield

got to make
Somerfield
Sorry can't stay
Heading Hoon Hay
Halswell
  Refuel
    All's well
      Duvauchelle.

STUART PAYNE

Encounter

in Cathedral
Square I am

stopped by a
fat American

clad completely
in black who

asks me where
you can score

some drugs &
what can you

actually do in
this country

anyway

JONATHAN FISHER

Filling Up

In this city the signposts
stare at empty fields; drivers
    detour from the weekdays
    to pull up in front of
        weatherboard churches -
    radiators are filled
        with holy water.

On this inexplicable
day light discharges over
    the PORT-A-LOO. Workmen
    gutter their waxed lunchwrap
        and tar-seal their butts
    for posterity. ...*Fuck*
        the thermos is bust...

Yes. From this to this to that
and then? All those connections
    missed. You did. Take the car
    and skid through the skyline —
        why are there no stars
    why are there so many
        you still can't answer?

DAVID HOWARD

& still

A hawk on eddy & easy, over open country
Its wing's sheen a poplar leaf's
flickered natter-sampled
on each scythed stroke sunward

& light —

rolling this blue Bic pen onto a splinter
my thumbprint acquired several days ago,
off a window flanking Sumner,
on bottle smooth & aquamarine,
white hot
& *noli me tangere* —
walking toward Cave Rock,
in light, reading the damp sand

From under a blue haze beneath Mount Grey,
here there be petrol heads
around three AM —

PM

& Takahe

& Kiwi

& Bellbird ...
We read the Crater's lip
You remember horizontal Welsh rain
I say Quail Island's like Onawe

but the isthmus is sundered

& Peter got out of the boat
& without trace,
along the line of control —
One Nation
& in Cornwall his assertion places you
in a Table of Kindred and Affinity

& in London Street — spicy apple cake
                    bacon n' egg sandwiches
                    one white cup of tea
                    one black ...
& red stone walls made convicts free
          & my great, great grandfather
James Reston was Governor of the Lyttelton Gaol
& time holds the ball down
& still the light
& still

ERIC MOULD

Contributors and Sources

John Allison was born in Blenheim in 1950. He lived in Christchurch for 30 years before moving to Melbourne in 2001, where he works as an education consultant. Publications include *Dividing the Light*, Hazard Press 1997; *Both Roads Taken*, Sudden Valley Press, 1997; *Stone Moon Dark Water*, Sudden Valley Press 1999.

'Bridge of Remembrance', *Poetry New Zealand 14*; 'West Melton' and 'Suburban Street', *Both Roads Taken*, Sudden Valley Press, 1997.

Lorna Staveley Anker (1914-2000) was born and educated in Christchurch before moving north on her marriage. The family returned to Christchurch and she began writing in her 50s. She published three books of poetry and her work has been represented in local and international anthologies.

'Yet More Words', *A Particular Stave*, published by the author, 1993.

Jennifer Barrer was born into a Canterbury family involved in the arts and mountains for over 100 years. An actress and director, her poetry collections include *Te Rangianiwaniwa* (Nag's Head Press, 1988), *Follow the Sun* (Hazard Press, 1992) and *Looking Up* (Caxton, 1997). She was awarded a Winston Churchill Fellowship in 1996.

'Christchurch', *Follow the Sun*, Hazard Press, 1992.

Helen Bascand is active in the Christchurch poetry community. Her work has appeared in several poetry magazines and anthologies and has been placed and commended in Australian and New Zealand competitions. Her collection *windows on the morning side* was published in 2001.

'Light & silent singing', *windows on the morning side*, Sudden Valley Press, 2001.

Blanche Baughan (1870-1958) was born in England where she grew up, was educated and became a suffragette. She moved to New Zealand in 1902. After some time in the North Island, she moved to Banks Peninsula and, apart from a period in Sumner, lived the remainder of her life in Akaroa. She was a well-known and prolific poet up until the 1920s, her two notable books being *Single-Short and Other Verses* (1908) and *Poems for the Port Hills* (1923).

'A Bush Section', *An Anthology of Twentieth Century New Zealand Verse* selected by Vincent O'Sullivan, Oxford University Press, 1970.

Born in England, **Ursula Bethell** (1874-1945) came to New Zealand as a small child when her parents settled in Rangiora. She returned to Europe to complete her education and did not return permanently for 25 years, when she bought Rise Cottage on the Cashmere Hills. It was from here, amidst her beloved garden and the views of the plains and mountains, that she wrote the bulk of her celebrated poetry. Her *Collected Poems* was published posthumously in 1950.

'By the River Ashley', 'Gale SSW', 'October Morning', and 'Pause' from *Collected Poems*, Oxford University Press, 1985.

Earle Birney (1904-1995) This celebrated Canadian poet was widely travelled and visited New Zealand and Australia in the early 1970s. He was born in Calgary and was a recipient of the Governor-General's Award for his poetry, which was colloquial and vigorous, often espousing his radical social and political views.

'Christchurch, NZ', *Ghost in the Wheels; Selected Poems*, McLelland & Stewart, Toronto, 1977.

Victoria Broome is a psychiatric social worker in the Family Mental Health Service. She has published widely in New Zealand literary journals and is currently the poetry editor of *Takahe*.

'Don't Draw the Curtains', *Takahe 37*, 1999; 'My Aunts in the 1960s', previously unpublished.

James Brown lives in Wellington with his partner and two daughters. His books of poetry are *Go Round Power Please* (Victoria University Press, 1995), *Lemon* (Victoria University Press, 1999) and *Favourite Monsters* (Victoria University Press, 2002). He was the Writer in Residence at the University of Canterbury in 2001.

'Loneliness', *The Press*.

Greeba Brydges-Jones, born and bred in Christchurch, has a life-long love of the Port Hills. A retired teacher, interests include writing, reading, gardening, canoeing, walking and long discussions with literary friends over several cappuccinos. Has work published in New Zealand, Australia, England, Japan and America. 'Port Hills Mid-Summer' was second in the New Zealand Poetry Society competition in 1993.

'Port Hills Mid-Summer', *Black before the Sun*, NZ Poetry Society, 1993.

D'Arcy Cresswell (1896-1960), who spent most of his life in self-imposed exile on the fringes of the English literary scene, wrote poetry that was defiantly backward-looking and romantic. Born and educated in Canterbury, he is read today mainly for his prose memoirs and his letters.

'Sonnet XVIII' *from* 'Lyttelton Harbour', *A Book of New Zealand Verse 1923-1945* chosen by Allen Curnow, Caxton Press, 1945.

Allen Curnow (1895-1960) was one of the leading figures in twentieth-century New Zealand literature. He was not only a fine poet but also the influential editor of two important anthologies which helped establish the direction of poetry in New Zealand. He was born and raised in Canterbury and spent some years as a journalist on *The Press*. He was awarded the Order of New Zealand in 1990.

Permission to reproduce 'The Old Provincial Council Buildings, Christchurch', 'The Skeleton of the Great Moa in the Canterbury Museum, Christchurch', and 'Wild Iron,' courtesy of the copyright owner Jeny Curnow c/- Tim Curnow, Literary Consultant, Sydney.

Gregory Dally was born in Waiuku and now lives in Christchurch. He has been published in *JAAM, Meanjin, Sport* and other journals.

'Flippers', *Takahe 41*, 2001.

Basil Dowling (1910-?) was born in Southbridge and educated at Canterbury University. Although he left New Zealand to teach in England in the early fifties, much of his poetry is concerned with his Christchurch boyhood. He published eight collections of poetry, his early work with the Caxton Press.

'Canterbury Nor'Wester', *The Penguin Book of New Zealand Verse*, 1960.

Joan Drewery lives and writes in Christchurch.

'Drought', *The Press*, 2001

David Eggleton is a Dunedin poet, writer and critic who has published four books of poems. His most recent projects include two poetry-based short films, and the collaborative 12-track poetry album *CC Versifier*.

'Self-criticism of an Otago Poetry Worker', *South Pacific Sunrise* (Penguin 1986).

David Elworthy was born in South Canterbury and educated in Christchurch and England. After 10 years in the New Zealand diplomatic service he turned to book publishing. He now runs Shoal Bay Press in partnership with his wife, Ros Henry. His work has appeared in *Landfall*, *The Listener*, and the first *Penguin Book of New Zealand Verse*.

'Afternoon Tea', *Landfall*, 1954.

Rangi Faith is from South Canterbury, of Kai Tahu descent. He is a teacher by profession and currently lives in Rangiora. Publications include *Dangerous Landscapes*, Longman Paul; *Unfinished Crossword*, Hazard Press 1990; and *Rivers Without Eels*, Huia Press, 2001.

'A Good Place', *Rivers Without Eels* , Huia Press, 2001.

Fiona Farrell was born in Oamaru and educated at Otago and in Toronto. She has been writing since the 1980s. To date she has published two books of poetry, two collections of short stories and three novels. Her novel *The Skinny Louie Book* won the New Zealand Book Award for Fiction in 1992, and she has won many other awards, including the Bruce Mason Award for Playwrights and the Katherine Mansfield Fellowship in Menton.

'Penguins', *The Press*.

Kenneth Fea's poetry and prose has been widely published in New Zealand, Australia, the UK and the USA. His collection of poems *on what is not* was published in 1999 by Sudden Valley Press.

'Poem with Epigraph', *Voiceprints 2*, Canterbury Poets Collective.

Jonathan Fisher is a widely published poet who lives and writes in Christchurch. He was the editor of 'When Two Men Embrace', the gay section of *The New Zealand Anthology of Gay and Lesbian Poetry*. His first collection, *the sun is darker*, will be published early in 2003.

'Encounter', *The Press*; 'I Remember South Brighton', *Borderlands*, Giant Press, 1995.

Catherine Fitchett is a Wellington-born poet. Twenty years' residence in Christchurch, not to mention many childhood holidays, allow her to count herself as almost a

Cantabrian. After training as a scientist, and raising a family of young writers, she now writes, works in accounts and researches genealogy.

'Fresh Bread', *The Press*, 2000.

Christina Fitchett is a young Christchurch poet. She has attended classes at the Christchurch School for Young Writers for several years. She takes most of her inspiration from her surroundings.

'Russet Rain', *And Me for all of Those. Voices of Canterbury*, Clerestory Press, 2000

Denis Glover (1912-1980). The colourful figure of Denis Glover will not only always be associated with his canonical poem 'The Magpies' but also with his great sequences *Sings Harry* and *Arawata Bill*. He was educated at Canterbury University and in the thirties established the Caxton Press, which became a nursery for many writers who later became major literary figures.

'For a Child', *Anthology of New Zealand Verse*, Oxford University Press, 1956; 'The Magpies', *Enter Without Knocking*, Pegasus Press, 1964. Published with the permission of the Granville Glover Family Trust.

David Gregory is a Christchurch-based poet. He is a founder member of the Christchurch Poets Collective and is active in the promotion of poetry through performance and publication. Among his publications are two collections of poetry, *Always Arriving* and *Frame of Mind*, both published by Sudden Valley Press.

'Signs Taken for Wonders', *And Me for all of Those*, Clerestory Press, 2000; 'You Are Here', *Always Arriving*, Sudden Valley Press, 1997.

Bernadette Hall is an award-winning poet whose fifth collection of poems, *Settler Dreaming*, was published by Victoria University Press in 2001. In 1991 she was Writer in Residence at the University of Canterbury and in 1996 held the Burns Fellowship at Otago. For ten years she was poetry editor of *Takahe* and is currently poetry editor for *The Press*. She teaches Latin at Christchurch Girls High School.

'Open Field', *Settler Dreaming*, Victoria University Press, 2001; 'Plainsong I', *Heartwood,* Caxton Press, 1989; Party Tricks', *The Persistent Levitator*, Victoria University Press, 1994; 'Windsurfing', *Of Elephants etc*, Untold Press 1990.

Michael Harlow has published six books of poetry, most recently *Giotto's Elephant*, which was a finalist in the National Book Awards in 1991. He has also published short prose in various literary periodicals and anthologies. He was the Katherine Mansfield Memorial Fellow to Menton, France in 1986. At present he lives and works in Central Otago as a writer and Jungian analytical psychotherapist. He has just completed a collection of poems and short prose, *Cassandra's Daughter*.

'And Just Now', *Vlaminck's Tie*, Auckland University Press/Oxford University Press, 1985; 'Not Less by Dreaming More' and 'The Conversation of Things', *Today is the Piano's Birthday*, Auckland University Press/Oxford University Press, 1981.

Jeffrey Harpeng is a co-founder and long-term stalwart of the Canterbury Poets Collective and a member of the Small White Teapot Haiku Group and the Lost Friday Salon, an editorial group. His current literary fixations are writing sonnets and haibun.

'January Child', *The Press*, 2001.

Jeffrey Paparoa Holman was born in London in 1947 and came to New Zealand in 1950. He grew up on naval bases and, praise be, Te Tai Poutini, the West Coast. His lifelong obsessions are his absent sailor father and the Blackball Bridge. He is presently a thesis student in the Māori Department at the University of Canterbury, researching the work of Elsdon Best.

'The secret life of Arana Kohu Rau' is previously unpublished.

David Howard co-founded the literary quarterly *Takahe* in 1989, edited the critical miscellany *Complete With Instructions* (Firebrand, 2001) and compiled *Shebang: Collected poems 1980-2000* for Steele Roberts (2000). His collaboration with the photographer Fiona Pardington, *How To Occupy Ourselves*, is forthcoming from Steele Roberts. 'Filling Up' was first published in *Printout No. 4*, 1993.

Isobelle Hudson was born in Christchurch in 1920. She has been painting and draw-ing all her life but developed a latent love of poetry when attending creative writing classes after doing UE English and Art History at Hagley High, as an adult student in her late 50s. 'Leaf' was first published in *The Press* in 2001.

Jan Hutchison lives in Christchurch. A collection of her poems, *The Long Sleep is Over*, was published by Steele Roberts, 1999. She is represented in various anthologies including *New Zealand Love Poems* and publications such as *Coastlines*.

'A Lesson on the Beach', *The Long Sleep is Over*, Steele Roberts, 1999; 'Cul-de-Sac with Chestnut Trees and Small Asian Woman', previously unpublished.

Rob Jackaman was born in the east of England and has lived in New Zealand since 1972. He teaches modern poetry and creative writing at the University of Canterbury, and is editor of the Hazard Press Australasian Poets series. He is currently awaiting the publication of his thirteenth book of poems.

'Quail Island / Connection', *Distances*, Hazard Press 1992; 'Yeats in Clarence Street', *Late Love Songs*, Hazard Press, 2001.

Helen Jacobs is the pen-name of Elaine Jakobsson. She has had four collections of poetry published as well as poems in many magazines and anthologies. She has been living in Christchurch for the past eight years and is currently the chairperson of the Canterbury Poets Collective.

'Frost' and 'Hill Walk', *Pools Over Stone*, Sudden Valley Press, 1997; 'Without Icons', *The Old Moon And So On*, Poetry Society, 1994.

Karalyn Joyce has had poetry published in magazines such as *The Listener*, *Takahe*, and *North & South*, plus work in anthologies such as John Gordon's *Fresh Fields* and *The New Zealand Collection of Poetry & Prose*. 'Rural Downtown', first published in *The Press*, is about living and writing in small town Pleasant Point.

Laura Joyce is a young Christchurch writer of much promise. 'Townies' was written while she was a student at St Andrew's College and published in the millennium collec-tion *And Me for all of Those* (Clerestory Press).

Jan Kemp Riemenschneider. Since publication of her fifth volume of poems *Only One Angel* (University of Otago Press, 2001), Jan Kemp has been collecting recordings of New Zealand poets for the SCAPA Archive. 'At Taylor's Mistake' was first published in *Diamonds and Gravel* (Hampson Hunt, 1979) and written during a visit to Christchurch in 1975.

Koenraad Kuiper, who emigrated from the Netherlands in 1951, teaches linguistics at the University of Canterbury. His poetry has been published in a number of literary magazines such as *Islands, Landfall, Poetry New Zealand, Sport* and *Takahe*. He has published three books of poetry, the latest, *Timepieces*, in the Hazard Poets Series.

'The white funeral at Marken', *Poetry New Zealand No. 5*, 1992.

Hugh Lauder was born in Germany of Australian parents. He moved to New Zealand in 1978, where he lectured in education before becoming Professor of Education at Victoria University, Wellington. During his time in this country he edited *Landfall* for some time and published two collections of poetry with the Caxton Press: *Over the White Wall* (1985) and *Knowledge of the Left Hand* (1990).

'Two Pictures by Van der Velden', *Knowledge of the Left Hand*, Caxton Press, 1990.

Graham Lindsay has published six books of poems. A new book, *Lazy Wind Poems*, is due from Auckland University Press in 2003. He edited, designed and published the literary periodical *Morepork* in 1979-80. He recently participated in the Seeing Voices poetry festival in Auckland, and is currently working on an extended prose poem.

'Sunset', 'Taylors Mistake' and 'Tourist Times', *Legend of the Cool Secret*, Sudden Valley Press, 1999.

Joy Lowe

'First Perceptions', *Takahe 14*, 1993.

Owen Marshall has written or edited 18 books. He received the ONZM for services to literature in the Queen's New Year Honours, 2000, and his novel *Harlequin Rex* won the Montana Book Awards Deutz Medal for fiction. In 2002 the University of Canterbury awarded him the honorary degree of Doctor of Letters.

'Pukeko', *The Press*, 2002.

Barbara McCartney works in a Christchurch medical consultancy. She wrote poetry as a child and started again in 1998. She has had work published in *Poetry NZ*, *Takahe*, and *The Press*.

'Avon River at Carlton Mill', *Poetry New Zealand No. 19*, 1999.

Frankie McMillan is a Christchurch writer. She is currently working on a novel but sometimes gets sidetracked by other literary forms such as poetry. 'Developing my Father' was published in 2002 by *The Press*.

Born in Little River, **Harvey McQueen** grew up on Banks Peninsula. Graduating from Canterbury University he went secondary school teaching and has worked in education all his life. He has had five volumes of poetry published and is a well-known anthologist, co-editing the successful *Penguin Book of New Zealand Verse*.

'Port Levy Hilltop', *Against the Maelstrom*, Caxton Press, 1981.

Mike Minehan lives in a small coastal community north of Christchurch. First published in 1972 in university magazines and *Broadsheet*, she began writing full-time in 1988. She has had poems published in *Metro*, *Island (Australia)*, *Poetry NZ*, *Ariel* and many other literary magazines and anthologies. Her first book *No Returns* was published in 1989 and since then she has published five others including the most recent, a memoir, *Oh Jerusalem*.

'in camera', *Printout No. 4*, 1993.

Eric Mould was born in Akaroa in 1958. Ko Onawe te taonga. Resident in Rangiora, the father of Hugh, and working at a horticultural nursery, Eric is a committee member of the Canterbury Poets Collective, deputy editor of Poets Group, the sister press of Sudden Valley Press. He is also involved in the Lost Friday Salon, the Small White Teapot Haiku Group, and addicted to most things poetic.

'Continuity' and '& still' are previously unpublished.

Born in Blenheim, **John Newton** graduated M.A. from the University of Canterbury and PhD from the University of Melbourne. In 1985 his first collection, *Tales from the Angler's Eldorado*, was published by Untold Press. His poems have appeared in numerous anthologies including *The Penguin Book of Contemporary New Zealand Poetry* (1989) and *An Anthology of New Zealand Poetry in English*, Oxford, 1997. He teaches in the English Department at the University of Canterbury.

'The Sunshine Factory', *Tales from the Angler's Eldorado*, Untold Press, 1985.

James Norcliffe was born in 1946 in Greymouth but, apart from extended periods in Asia, has lived in Christchurch most of his life, currently teaching in Foundation Studies, Lincoln University. He has published a collection of short stories, children's novels and four collections of poetry, the most recent being *Letters to Dr Dee* (shortlisted for the NZ Book Awards 1994), *A Kind Of Kingdom* (Victoria University Press, 1998), and *Rat Tickling*, Sudden Valley Press, 2002. He was the 2000 Robert Burns Fellow at the University of Otago.

'above the estuary' and 'up on Waltham Bridge', *A Kind of Kingdom*, Victoria University Press, 1998; 'Birdlings Flat/Motukarara', *And Me for all of Those*, Clerestory Press, 2000.

John O'Connor's last book of poetry, *A Particular Context*, was voted one of the five best books of New Zealand poetry of the 1990s by members of the Poetry Society. He is a past winner of the NZPS International Prize, an occasional editor of small magazines, and managing editor of Sudden Valley Press.

'Home River', *The Press*, 1999; 'The Royal Visit', *A Particular Contrast*, Sudden Valley Press 1999.

Stuart Payne lives in Opawa and works part-time for the NZ Orienteering Federation. He has published a social history of road running in Canterbury as well as having short stories, plays and poems for children published in the *New Zealand School Journal*, other magazines, on radio and TV.

'Heading Hoon Hay', *New Zealand School Journal 1988, Part 4, No. 1* (on behalf of the Ministry of Education).

Joanna Preston is an expatriate Australian and born-again Cantabrian. She is a member of the Small White Teapot Haiku Group, the Lost Friday Salon and the Canterbury Poets' Collective. She recently edited *A Savage Gathering*, the 2002 NZPS competition anthology.

'Ebb', *The Press*, 2001.

Born in New Zealand, **Sarah Quigley** has a D.Phil. from the University of Oxford and lives in Berlin. She writes fiction and poetry and her new novel *Shot* will be published by Virago in 2003. Recent awards include the Burns Fellowship and the CLL Writer's Award.

'Sleeping Over', *Auckland University Press New Poets 1*, AUP, 1999.

Dave Robertson lives with his wife, cat and dogs on a precarious spit washed by the Pacific Ocean and the Avon-Heathcote Estuary. He completed the University of Canterbury's inaugural poetry writing paper in 1996. His work has previously been accepted for publication in *Takahe*, *The Listener* and *The Press*.

'Estuary Song', *The Press*, 2001.

Jane Simpson is a poet, historian, composer, and sometime university lecturer in religious studies. Her first poetry collection, *Candlewick kelp* (2002), comes out of a collaboration with the Christchurch sculptor, Bing Dawe. Since 2000 she has written poetry and music together, resulting in her CD *Tussocks Dancing*.

'Large Soaring Bird', *Candlewick kelp*, Christchurch Poets Group, 2002.

Elizabeth Smither is the current Te Mata Poet Laureate. Her new collection *Road Shows* will appear in March 2003, published by Godwit.

Professor Musgrove's Canary, Auckland University Press, 1986.

Barbara Strang was born in Invercargill, the oldest of ten children. She now lives at McCormacks Bay, Christchurch. She has had poems, haiku, short stories and children's writing published, and her first collection of poetry, *Duck Weather*, will appear soon. She has an M.A. in Creative Writing from Victoria University.

'Flowers Track', *The Press*, 1999.

Mervyn Thompson (1935-1992) was born in Otago and raised on the West Coast. After a period as a coal miner, he studied at Canterbury University where he developed his love of the stage and where he became a teacher and an author/director at the early Court Theatre. The selection in the book is an extract from his late autobiographical play *Passing Through*, a work of poetic intensity and grim humour (Hazard Press, 1992).

Louise Tomlinson lives and works in Christchurch.

'Gorge Hill', *The Press*, 1999.

Patsy Turner lives up Takamatua Valley and works at the Akaroa Museum. Her poetry has been performed at festivals and literary events and published in various anthologies. She is a founder member of the Canterbury and Banks Peninsula Poetry collectives. At present she is attempting to develop a relationship with the bass trombone.

'Onawe', *And Me for all of Those*, Clerestory Press, 2000; 'The Heroines', *Voice-prints 2*, Canterbury Poets Collective, 1995.

Hone Tuwhare was born in 1922 in Kaikohe. He belongs to Ngapuhi hapu, Ngati Korokoro, Ngati Tautahi and Te Popoto. In 1964 he published the enormously successful *No Ordinary Sun*. A dozen collections have followed, including *Mihi*, his collected poems, in 1987. In 1999 Hone Tuwhare was appointed the second Te Mata Estate Poet Laureate. He lives at Kaka Point, South Otago.

'Bus Journey, South', *Sap-wood & Milk*, Caveman Press, 1972.

Arnold Wall (1869-1966) was Professor of English for many years at the University of Canterbury and a prolific journalist. He published ten collections of traditional verse, many of the poems dealing with the Canterbury landscape.

'The City from the Hills', 'The City in the Plains', *The Penguin Book of New Zealand Verse*, 1960.

Tom Weston published *The Ambiguous Companion* in 1996. Since then his work has continued to appear in journals such as *Landfall* and *Sport*.

'Flying into Christchurch', *The Ambiguous Companion*, Hazard Press, 1996; 'I Would Be Seamstress', *The Press*, 2002.

Tim Whale. Fresh on the scene in 2002, Tim's poetry has been published by *The Press* and the Canterbury University Press. Tim loves Christchurch with a passion.

'Ae I eye' *The Press*.

Wensley Willcox grew up in Christchurch, where she attended school and university. She spent the first decade of her married life in Lincoln before moving to Auckland where she worked as a journalist and is now actively involved in the NZ Society of Authors (PEN NZ Inc.)

'Canterbury on a Cloudless Day', *A Woman in Green*, Steele Roberts, 2001.

Born in 1948, **Nick Williamson** grew up at Takapuna. He was educated at Auckland and Canterbury Universities and works as a probation officer. He lives in an old, two-storied house in central Christchurch with his dog, Josh, and his friend, Madame Yeti. His first book of poems, *The Whole Forest* was published in 2001.

'I Had this Vision', 'Recordings', 'South Brighton Love Song', *The Whole Forest*, Sudden Valley Press, 2001

Andrew Paul Wood was born in Timaru and educated at Otago, Massey and Canterbury Universities. Widely published as a poet and art historian within New Zealand, in various magazines and periodicals, he lived in Dunedin for seven years before moving to Christchurch, where he was Arts Editor for *Canta* and Christchurch correspondent for the now defunct *LOG Illustrated*. He works in the heritage industry.

'Eclogue: Christchurch in Winter' is previously unpublished.